The Romance

by Jason Shelley

The Romance

by Jason Shelley

TLÖN BOOKS

By the same author
No Looking Back
Grey Love

The Romance

First published in 2005 by
Tlön Books Publishing Ltd, London SE1 6TE

www.tlon.co.uk

Artwork by **Vishal Shah**
Book design by **Vishal Shah** and **Jason Shelley**
www.vishalshah.co.uk

ISBN 0954146824

Printed and bound in Great Britain by **Creative Print and Design Group**

A CIP record of this book is available from the British Library.

*On page 14 there is a deliberate spelling mistake - 'that' is spelt as 'taht'.

Absolutely no fucking, no cocks, allowed in this prose. Let us get this straight right from the beginning. This is going out in the year 2005. I am writing about what I know. This isn't much. This is something people will not want to read. The absolute complete bullshit. Someone ranting on about complete bullshit.

Well, anyway, I know what Judith wants. She wants pleasure.
She is out to get things, to appreciate things. What am I out to do, I wonder.

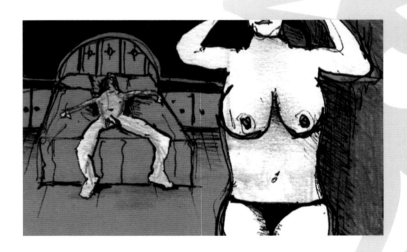

I am out to avoid paying the stupid debt that I have. I hate my debt. I hate it. I shouldn't have told my bank that I took a weekend in Milan. I shouldn't have told them that.

The intelligence of Martin seems to enable him to rise above anything. He could reach absolute poverty, then still deal with his bad poverty. He is poverty stricken. I am writing off the top of my skull. The top of my skull.

I am expressing myself truly, greatly. What I am writing is something you cannot stop me from writing. Grammatical mistakes. What are they? You cannot stop me from writing this. No one will ever read this, so what is the point.

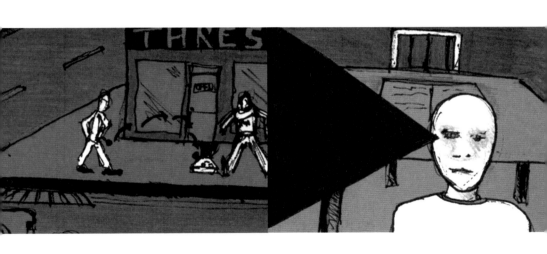

The point is that I don't know what else to do with myself.
This is absolute honesty. It isn't. it is slightly filtered.

15

What position am I in life. I don't know. I could be in a low position. If I am in a low position, I could rise above it with my writing. That would be suitable. How could I write? I am writing with very little. I don't know many words. Taht is an advantage. I am not stopping myself. I am throwing my full at you. I am throwing my full at you. Take that and that. I am injured. half my body is here. This half I am using is wounded. I am finding it hard to fight. There is stamina in there. I am trying to move quickly. I am working you out; you're moving up and down. So am I. This word means that. that word means this. Take that and that and that. I am not holding myself back. It is you and me only. My hands will not stop

I forgot to say; earlier I almost began crying. I have not disciplined myself for it to be absolute agony. it is agony. It is agony. the disciplined writer. It is better to write prose. It is better for you. It is good for you.

W here am I? I am living in South london, in a flat above a
shop on Walworth Road. i share this flat with two people;
one is Scottish, she got home from work, the hospital, at
10 o'clock. I wasn't here at that time. when I got in at
10.30 pm she was in typing away on a computer.
I am upstairs now.

It is, maybe, fifteen minutes past midnight. I have had some coffee and some toast, just recently. Do you really want to know the ins and outs of life. Do you really? The ins and outs of Jason Shelley. Do you want to know about it? I just heard one of my housemates make noise. It was half cough, half sneeze. I am now typing more quietly. I'm glad the way I write is restricted by the amount of words I know and by my knowledge of how to write. I don't think i know how to write.

It is not as bad as I would like it be. Again, I almost cry. when can I stop? I've been running for too long. I am not dehydrated. I'm glad that I am not. I am glad I am not. If I were something good might happen. You might see me fall down. I'd fall, my throat dry. My legs would give. I would fall, crashing to the ground. My knee would hit the concrete. It would bruise and graze. People give up. They accept what they have.

To write you just have to write. Some would argue differently. this writing is not as bad as I would like it to be.

I am determined to continue. I will get more. I will walk up a hill. i will collect energy. The hill is not there. I am nowhere. I am somewhere that is dry. I am somewhere that is wet. It is raining. I do not care. it is raining. The water falls onto me. I do not care. i am talking about nothing. I am talking about something. I am talking about myself.

Help me to get out of this. I do not want help. I don't need it.
I do need help. I don't need help out of something. I am not caught
in something. Kiss me. Kiss me. She kissed me.

Y̶ou almost saw me stop then. I will not stop. You cannot make me stop. You cannot. Keep way. Keep away. This is me. This is me. I am stopping. That is it. For now that is it. You cannot make me go on. This is my confession. I have no confession to give. SJSJAKE LLOS. YOSL MCNR GJAUD. That makes more sense.

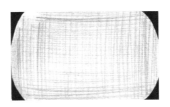

The End